MEET ALL THESE FRIENDS IN BUZZ BOOKS:

Thomas the Tank Engine
The Animals of Farthing Wood
Biker Mice From Mars
James Bond Junior
Fireman Sam
Joshua Jones
Rupert
Babar

First published in Great Britain 1994 by Buzz Books,
an imprint of Reed Children's Books
Michelin House, 81 Fulham Road, London SW3 6RB
and Auckland, Melbourne, Singapore and Toronto

ISBN 1 85591 448 4

Printed in Italy by Olivotto

The blue foxes looked in the pond.

"No Toad. No herons," said Scarface.

They went to the rabbit warren.

"Gone."

They looked under stones, in holes, and through the long grass.

"I know where they all are," growled Scarface. "Follow me."

"Charmer!" snapped Fox. "Is this true?"

"Y-yes, Father," said Charmer.

Fox was furious. "My own daughter!" he said bitterly. "Turning against us!"

"Ranger's not like Scarface," said Charmer. "He wants us all to be friends."

"We'll see," said Fox grimly.

Charmer wanted to look for Ranger. She crept towards the entrance of the earth.

"Stop her, Father," said Friendly. "She might betray us! She's been meeting Scarface's son, Ranger, in secret."

18

"Ridiculous! You weren't even born there," said Owl.

"But my father, Mole, was," said Mossy.

"Shh!" said Hare, his long ears pressed against the wall of the earth. "I can hear something. Scarface is getting closer!"

"Our enemy is strong and cunning," Fox said, "but he's going to find out that the animals of Farthing Wood still have the courage that made them famous!"

"Three cheers for Farthing Wood!" cried Mossy the mole.

"Hide in Fox's earth!" they called to the
Farthing Wood animals. "Hurry!"

The rabbits bolted out of their warren.
Toad hopped out of his pond. Whistler
and his mate, Speedy, glided down. Soon,
all of the animals had arrived.

"Kestrel! Owl!" barked Fox. "Call all the Farthing Wood animals together! Scarface will dig out their holes and burrows. The safest place for everyone is in my earth."

Owl and Kestrel flew off at once.

Hare was lying in the long grass nearby.
He heard Scarface's cruel plan. Quickly,
he ran back to tell Fox and the others.

"Oh dear," wailed Father Rabbit. "I'm
dying of fright already!"

"Don't panic!" squealed Mother Rabbit.

"Scarface won't get me!" cried Weasel.
"I'll hide!"

"Me too!" said Weasel's mate, Measly.

"You don't need to hide," said Weasel.
"You're not from Farthing Wood."

"We're going to catch every single
Farthing Wood animal we can find," he
said, "and drive them out of White Deer
Park. Then the park will be ours again."

"But Father," began Ranger.

"What's the matter, Son? Are you
scared?" growled Scarface.

11

Lady Blue had run back to Scarface.

"She went for me! That red vixen
attacked me for no reason!"

"Leave it to me," Scarface growled. "I'll
sort out those Farthing Wood creatures
once and for all!"

He called the bravest blue foxes together.

"You're hurt!" said Fox when he saw Vixen. "What happened?"

"Lady Blue attacked me," whispered Vixen, flopping down, exhausted.

Fox licked her wounds.

"I should have fought Scarface years ago," he said, "and I'm not going to put it off any longer!"

In another part of the wood, two young
foxes were smiling fondly at each other.

"You do love me, Charmer, don't you?"
asked Lady Blue's son.

"Oh, Ranger, of course I do," replied
Vixen's daughter.

"If only our parents were friends,"
sighed Ranger.

"This is Farthing land," said Vixen. "You have no right here."

"We'll see about that!" snarled Lady Blue, and she rushed at Vixen with bared teeth.

The fight was short. Lady Blue bit Vixen's neck and Vixen tore Lady Blue's ear.

"You'll pay for this!" yelped Lady Blue, skulking away.

Vixen lay in the summer sunshine.
Suddenly, she heard a noise, and
Lady Blue stepped out of the bushes.

"Grr," growled Vixen. "Go away!"

"I'm a blue fox," said Lady Blue,
"and I'll walk where I choose."

Showdown

Story by Colin Dann
Text by Mary Risk
Illustrations by The County Studio

"There's no point in going any further, Father," said Ranger. "They're not here. I'm sure of it."

Scarface snarled at him.

"What's wrong with you, Ranger? You're not a coward, are you? No son of mine is afraid of a fight! Come to the front of the pack with me!"

They arrived at Fox's earth.

"The game is up, Fox!" called Scarface.
"You're surrounded! Come out, or we'll
keep you down there till you starve!"

Charmer barked, hoping Ranger would
hear her. He did.

"Charmer! Be careful!" he called.

"What are we going to do?" said Vixen.

"There's only one thing for it," said Fox.
"I'll challenge Scarface to fight me on his
own, one to one!"

Bravely, Fox left the safety of his earth.

"Your quarrel's with me, not with my family and friends, Scarface," he said. "I'll fight you on my own."

Scarface said nothing. His sons looked at him uncertainly.

"Afraid of me, are you?" said Fox.

"How dare you!" bellowed Scarface.

"Then fight," said Fox.

One by one, the rest of the Farthing Wood animals crept out of Fox's earth. They stood back and watched silently.

"Grr!" roared Scarface, and he leaped at Fox's throat.

The fight was long and bitter. The two
hardened foxes prowled around each
other, then closed in, biting and snapping.
Scarface was bigger and stronger, but Fox
was more cunning. He waited for Scarface
to make a mistake, then leapt at him,
toppled him over, and held him down on
the ground, so Scarface couldn't move.
Fox glared at his enemy.

26

"Kee!" called Kestrel suddenly. "The warden's coming! Run away!"

Fox let go of Scarface, who slunk off, angry and beaten, to lick his wounds.

"Hooray! We won!" shouted the animals.

"You should have killed him when you had the chance, Father," said Friendly.

"I'm sure Scarface will leave us alone, at least for a while," said Fox. "One day, this quarrel will end."

"Perhaps then you will accept Ranger,"
said Charmer hopefully.

"Perhaps," Fox answered. "I saw today
that Ranger has good intentions. It's
Scarface who causes us trouble."

Nobody saw Adder slip away.
"Leave Ssscarface to me," she hissed.